C

Selfish Sher Khan Punished

Once upon a time, there lived a family of wolves in the jungles of the Seeonee Hills.

One day, a jackal named Tabaqui visited Father Wolf. The others did not like Tabaqui because he was very naughty and cunning. But Father Wolf welcomed him and gave him some bones.

Tabaqui ate them hungrily. Then he said, "I have some bad news. Sher Khan, the tiger, has gone to attack the woodcutter today."

Father Wolf was worried. He said, "We are not supposed to hunt men. If Sher Khan kills the woodcutter, the villagers will come in search of him and trouble all of us."

Father Wolf told his wife what he had heard. She said, "Sher Khan should be punished for this. He is selfish. He is risking the peace of the whole jungle."

Suddenly, they heard a loud howl. Father Wolf said, "I know what the sound is. Sher Khan is hurt."

Very soon, Tabaqui came running and said, "Sher Khan has burnt his paw in the woodcutter's campfire. He is in deep pain."

Mother Wolf said, "Finally, the mischief-maker is punished. Now, there will be peace in the forest as Sher Khan will not be able to hunt for a few days."

Mother Wolf's Kindness

The next day, Father Wolf and Mother Wolf were sitting outside their cave when they heard a noise behind the bushes. To their great surprise, they saw a naked baby crawling out of the bushes.

Father Wolf cried, "It's a man cub!"

Mother Wolf said, "I have never seen a man cub. Please bring him to the cave."

Father Wolf gently picked him up in his mouth and carried him into the cave. Father Wolf and Mother Wolf were surprised to see that the baby was not afraid and was laughing! The baby started playing with their cubs straightaway.

Mother Wolf asked her husband, "Since he looks like a part of our family, can we keep him?"

Father Wolf looked shocked and asked, "Don't you think he would be a good meal for us?"

An annoyed Mother Wolf told her husband, "Like our babies, he too is someone's child. We should be kind to him. Also, see how lovable he looks!"

Father Wolf could not argue so he gave up and said, "He looks just like a little frog. I will call him Mowgli."

Mother Wolf was happy and felt proud of her husband.

Mother Wolf's Courage

A few days had passed since Sher Khan burnt his paw. One day, Tabaqui visited him and asked, "How are you feeling now?"

Sher Khan replied, "I am feeling much better now. After I attacked the woodcutter's family, they fled, but his little cub is missing."

Tabaqui, who loved to create trouble, said, "The man cub is with the Wolf family."

Sher Khan laughed and said, "Ha! He will make a wonderful meal for me!"

He then went and roared outside the Wolf's cave, "Return the man cub to me at once!"

Father Wolf said, "Go away! He is now a part of our family."

Sher Khan's eyes turned red with anger; he asked Father Wolf, "Have you forgotten that I can kill all of you in one go?"

Hearing this, Mother Wolf got ready to charge at Sher Khan. She said, "I am known for my strength and bravery. Now go away

or I shall teach you a lesson!"

Father Wolf said to his wife, "I am proud of you!"

She whispered, "If we look scared, he will try to bully us. Pretend to be stronger than him."

Sher Khan knew that it would be difficult to defend himself if Mother Wolf attacked as his paw was burnt. So, he backed out, growling.

Mowgli Is Accepted by All

According to the Jungle Law, all the wolf cubs had to be shown at the Council Rock during the monthly meeting. At times, other animals also gathered there.

Father Wolf and Mother Wolf took Mowgli along to the meeting. He played merrily with the other cubs when the meeting began.

Finally, Akela the leader of the wolf pack said, "Bring forward all the new-borns."

One by one, the wolves showed their cubs. Soon, it was Mowgli's turn. Father Wolf pushed him forward. The wolves looked at him in wonder, while Akela howled, "What are we supposed to do with a man cub?"

Father Wolf and Mother Wolf explained the story to their pack. Then, Akela said, "A family of wolves can keep a foreign creature only if two other animals vouch for him. Does anyone speak for the cub?"

Baloo, the brown bear, said, "I do. I will teach him the Jungle Law."

Bagheera, the black panther, also came forward and said, "I too vouch for Mowgli. I will give a bullock to the pack as the price for Mowgli to be a part of the group."

Father Wolf and Mother Wolf thanked Baloo and Bagheera. Thus, Mowgli became a part of the Seeonee wolf pack.

Bagheera's Story

Everyone in the jungle was scared of Bagheera. He was stronger and more respected than even Sher Khan.

Bagheera was born in a cage. His mother had been taken away from the jungle many years ago. She was caged and kept in the kingdom of Oodeypore (now Udaipur) in Rajasthan.

His mother longed to be free. One day, she said, "Son, I will soon die and will never be able to see the jungle again. But, if you ever get a chance to be free, go there."

Bagheera grew up in the cage. There, he got to know about human beings and their ways. He learnt a lot and became wise.

As Bagheera grew up, he became stronger. One day, he was not given food on time. He was very hungry and that made him very angry. Finally, he used all his strength and broke open the bars of the cage.

Then he escaped into the jungle, where

he found many members of the cat family.
They welcomed him and taught him the
ways and the laws of the jungle.

Now, he was the wisest amongst all of
them, as he knew the ways of man as well as
those of the jungle. He lived peacefully and
loved all the other animals.

Mowgli Helps the Wolf Cubs

Soon after he was adopted by the Wolf family, Mowgli felt completely at home in the jungle.

Father Wolf taught him how to hunt. The wolf cubs grew up very fast, but Mowgli still looked like a child. They lovingly made fun of him. Father Wolf and Mother Wolf loved Mowgli a lot and scolded their cubs when they teased him.

One day, the cubs left the cave to hunt. Mowgli begged them to let him come along. They laughed, "You are a little baby. Mother will scold us if you get hurt."

Mowgli was very sad. He did not want to be left behind. So, the eldest cub said, "Let us take him along. He might be of some help."

The others laughed at the idea but agreed, as they could not bear to see Mowgli upset.

On the way, the cubs stepped on a thorny bush by mistake. A few thorns stuck to their paws. They cried out in pain.

Mowgli calmed them down. He then took out the thorns from each cub's paws and eased the pain. They thanked Mowgli with all their hearts. They also promised to take him along on every hunt, and to never tease him again!

Mowgli Grows Up

Ten years passed and Mowgli grew up with the help of Father Wolf, Baloo and Bagheera. Soon, Mowgli learnt all the tricks of the jungle.

As promised, Baloo taught Mowgli the Jungle Laws. Mowgli learnt them fast and soon became Baloo's pet.

One day, Baloo was sitting under a tree and drinking honey from a pot. Just then, Mowgli came and asked, "What are you drinking?"

Baloo replied, "I am drinking honey. Try some."

Mowgli tasted some and was very happy. He cried, "I have never tasted anything as sweet as this! Where did you get it?"

Baloo said, "Honeybees collect honey in their hives on trees."

Mowgli asked, "Can't I climb the trees and get honey from the hives?"

A few monkeys were sitting on the tree. They heard the question and laughed at

Mowgli. They teased, "Mowgli, you can never learn to climb the trees like us!"

Bagheera heard the monkeys' boast from a distance.

He showed Mowgli the easiest way to climb trees.

Mowgli was a fast learner. Very soon, he could leap from one branch to the other. He sat on the branches and enjoyed drinking honey. The monkeys were ashamed.

Mowgli Learns to Be Punctual

One day, Mowgli was enjoying the sunshine outside his cave when Mother Wolf came to him and told him about the fortnightly meeting that day.

"Be on time. If you are late, it will annoy the leader and the other wolves," she warned.

Mowgli promised to be at the meeting on time. He then went to Baloo for his lessons. After his lessons, he roamed the jungle.

In the evening, Mowgli met Bagheera near the pond. Bagheera said, "What are you doing here? You should go for the meeting right now or you will be late."

"I will go soon," Mowgli said, carelessly.

Then, he sat on a rock and stared at the moon for a while. Suddenly, he realized that it was night and he was late! He ran to the meeting place.

Akela and the other wolves were very angry. They said, "You have no right to belong to our pack if you cannot follow our rules!"

Some wolves even hinted that Mowgli should be thrown out at once. Mother Wolf apologized for Mowgli and asked everyone to forgive him.

Mowgli felt ashamed that his mother had to do this. He apologized to everybody and decided to be on time in future.

Mowgli Saves Leela

Akela had a granddaughter named Leela who hated Mowgli.

Like many others, she felt that he should be thrown out. She always plotted with the other wolves to plead with Akela that Mowgli was not fit to be in their pack.

During one fortnightly meeting, she said, "Mowgli should prove his strength if he wants to continue living with us. He should compete with me and win."

Many wolves took Leela's side. So, Akela had no choice. He said, "Whoever is able to kill two rabbits and three birds by tomorrow evening will win."

Mowgli knew that it was a difficult task for him but he agreed to face the challenge. Leela was so keen on looking for prey and beating Mowgli that, without realizing, she went close to Sher Khan's den. Sher Khan heard her and came out.

Just as Sher Khan was about to attack Leela, Mowgli ran towards them and hit

Sher Khan with his wooden knife. Leela
jumped into the pond to save herself but
fainted and almost drowned. Mowgli
jumped in and saved her life. He took her to
Akela and told him what happened.

Akela thanked him, and Leela said
sorry too.

In the next meeting, Akela praised
Mowgli for saving Leela.

Mowgli's New Friend

One day, Mowgli was going to the river to drink water, when he found a little creature lying on the bank. The creature was out cold. So, Mowgli called Bagheera for help.

Bagheera looked at the creature and said, "This is a red panda. He is a rare animal and is found high up in the Himalayas. I wonder how he came here!"

Mowgli said, "I think he must have fallen in the river. The flow of water could have carried him here."

Baloo came there. He looked at the panda and said, "Mowgli, no one can live on this earth without friends. The more friends we make, the better it is. So, you must save this little creature."

Mowgli sprinkled a little water on the panda's face. He opened his eyes but he was too weak to get up. Mowgli ran to bring some eggs to feed him. He nursed the panda back to health and took him to his cave.

Mother Wolf was happy and said, "One must always be kind and gentle to other creatures. I am proud of you."

She took good care of him. The panda stayed in their cave till he became well.

Sher Khan's Trap

The panda, named Pappu, became healthy under Mowgli's care.

As soon as Pappu was fit to explore the jungle, he started following Mowgli wherever he went.

Very soon, the whole jungle learnt about Mowgli's and Pappu's close friendship.

One day, Tabaqui went to Sher Khan and said, "My Lord, I have found a great way to kill Mowgli. I can fool Pappu easily and bring him to your cave. Mowgli will surely come to save him."

Sher Khan thought this was a good plan and told Tabaqui to carry it out. The monkeys, who were Tabaqui's friends, promised to lure Pappu by giving him fruits.

Pappu fell into their trap. When they reached Sher Khan's cave, the monkeys left Pappu and scrambled away. Sher Khan came out and was about to attack him when Mowgli arrived there and hit Sher Khan with his knife.

Before Sher Khan could recover, Mowgli picked Pappu in his arms and ran away. Sher Khan followed them but, blind with anger, he fell into a pond.

Pappu thanked Mowgli for saving his life again. Mowgli said, "It is our duty to help our friends in times of need."

Baloo and Bagheera praised Mowgli for teaching Sher Khan a lesson.

Mowgli Learns Another Lesson

As time passed, Baloo and Bagheera became Mowgli's best friends.

One day, Mowgli was sitting with Bagheera.

Bagheera said, "Mowgli, I feel that you should not trust all the members of your pack."

Mowgli asked, "Why do you think so, Bagheera?"

He replied, "Akela is very old now. Sher Khan wants to gain from this and has made friends with some of the wolves. He wants to kill you and Akela."

Mowgli was shocked. He could not believe that the members of his own pack could plot against him. He said, "It is not possible, Bagheera. They are all my brothers."

Bagheera explained, "You must never trust others blindly."

Bagheera took Mowgli to the hill. Sher

Khan had called for a secret meeting with some wolves to get them on his side.

As Mowgli reached the hill, he heard the wolves say, "We are with you Sher Khan! We will hand over the man cub. Then, you can easily kill and eat him."

Mowgli hugged Bagheera and thanked him. He said, "You have opened my eyes in time. Now, I will always be careful."

Bagheera promised to help Mowgli whenever he needed him.

Mowgli Brings the Red Flower

When Mowgli came to know that some wolves were against him, he was very upset. He and Bagheera went to Baloo for advice. Mowgli hugged Baloo and cried, "I never thought that the members of my own pack would turn against me!"

Baloo calmed Mowgli. Then, he turned to Bagheera and said, "Bagheera, you have lived with men. Do you have any idea about what men use to scare animals?"

Bagheera replied, "We are all scared of the red flower (fire) that is seen outside the villagers' houses at night. Mowgli must get that red flower to be safe."

Baloo agreed and they sent Mowgli to the village.

In the village, Mowgli waited outside a hut and watched what the family did. He learnt how to light a fire and keep it burning. He stole a fire-pot and fled.

When he returned home, he told his

family about the other wolves' betrayal.
They were very upset.

Mowgli then showed them the red flower.
His family was startled to see it.

Mowgli promised, "I will use the red
flower only for my safety and never to hurt
anybody."

The family was thankful and blessed
Mowgli.

Mowgli Saves Akela's Life

One day, Sher Khan called the wolf pack for a meeting.

He saw Mowgli and roared, "I hate this man cub. He was my prey. Give him back to me!"

Akela was very angry. He said, "Sher Khan, you cannot give orders while I am alive."

Many members of the pack were on Sher Khan's side. They howled, "Mowgli does not belong to us. Give him to Sher Khan!"

Akela loved Mowgli. He said, "If he belongs to men, then let Mowgli go back to the village. We should not kill him."

Sher Khan became angrier. He spoke to the pack, "Your old leader is not even able to gather food for you. Kill him first!"

The pack knew that Akela was old and useless. They were ready to kill him and choose a new leader who could hunt for them.

Bagheera said to Mowgli, "Now is the time to use the red flower. Save Akela's life and your own!"

Mowgli stood up, holding a burning branch. He waved it at Sher Khan and the wolves.

Akela thanked Mowgli and said, "I am proud of you, my son!"

Mowgli Leaves the Jungle

Mowgli had never felt like a stranger in the jungle. But now he felt all alone. After he waved the sparkling red flower, making most of the wolves run, Mowgli sat with Akela and Bagheera.

He said, "I felt this jungle was my home and I belonged to the wolves. But everything has changed today. I neither belong to the wolves nor do I feel like a man."

Tears rolled down his cheeks and his heart was completely broken.

Bagheera hugged him and said, "Cry your heart out, little brother. I can understand what you are going through."

Mowgli said, "Bagheera, I must leave the jungle now. My brothers have cast me out."

Bagheera agreed with him, as he felt it was important for Mowgli's safety.

Mowgli returned home and told his family about his plans. Father Wolf and

Mother Wolf felt sorry for him and said,
"We understand why you want to leave right
now but you must come back soon. We love
you and will always wait for you."

Mowgli bid a sad goodbye to his family,
Bagheera, Akela and Baloo. Then, he
walked out of the jungle and into the world
of men.

Titles in

ILLUSTRATED

001–048

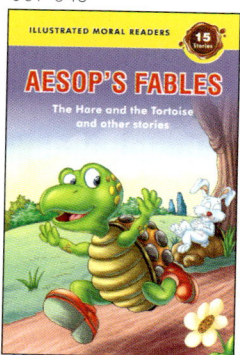

Aesop's Fables
SET OF 48 BOOKS

049–060

Akbar and Birbal
SET OF 12 BOOKS

061–080

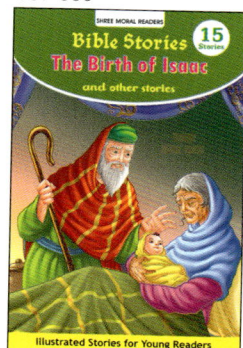

Bible Stories
SET OF 20 BOOKS

081–088

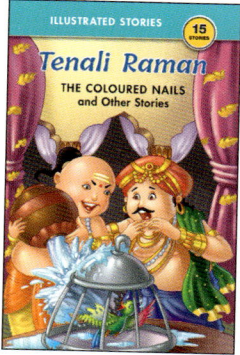

Tenali Raman
SET OF 8 BOOKS

089–094

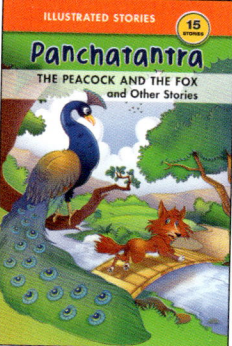

Panchatantra Stories
SET OF 6 BOOKS

095–114

Arabian Nights
SET OF 20 BOOKS